René Siegfried
Translated by Joel Mann

The Serif Fairy

Explorations in the World of Letters

Mark Batty Publisher · New York City

The Little Serif Fairy

The Serif Fairy was a clever little letter-fairy. Sometimes she was careless, and on one of her flying adventures she lost a wing – the left one, wouldn't you know it – the wing with which she could do magic. She hadn't even noticed at first. When she tried to chase after an especially beautiful butterfly, only then did she become aware of her predicament. She couldn't fly anymore. "It's no use," she said loudly, "I need my wing," and so began her search.

In Garamond Forest

At that very moment she discovered one of the most beautiful butterflies that she had ever seen. Whistling merrily, she skipped behind it. In the distance she could just see the first trees of Garamond Forest …

She meticulously searched the area and tried to remember where it had happened. She couldn't recall that unhappy moment when she had lost her wing. Wishing she, too, could fly again, she watched a bird as it fluttered through the air.

Deeper and deeper walked the little Serif Fairy into the dark woods, which before long consisted of nothing but tall fir trees. On the way she discovered a strange plant whose leaves moved gently in the wind. A strong gust of wind caused one of the leaves to fall off and sail softly to the ground.

"Just like a wing," thought the little letter-fairy, who by this time had almost forgotten that she was on a search for her magic wing. As if in a dream, she continued on and caught several glimpses of a majestic stag in a clearing. She thought about flying, about magic, indeed, about the lightness of being a letter-fairy and didn't notice that she had long since left the forest.

The Zentenar Gate

All around it was growing lighter, and the vastness of the landscape fascinated her no less than the great swarm of butterflies she encountered, which she longed to gaze at indefinitely. She climbed up into a hedge but was so occupied with the colorful butterflies that she failed to appreciate its beautiful shape until she had clambered down again.

Full of curiosity, she traipsed farther along until she came to a gigantic gate that looked like the sort of gate behind which a king would live – a king with tremendous power who might very well know where and how the Serif Fairy could recover her wing.

In front of the gate she met a dog, which came up to her, wagging its tail. Together they went through the Zentenar Gate – but of a king they saw not a trace.

"Sorry, my friend, but I have no time to play with you," said the letter-fairy.
"I am searching for my wing." Then the Serif Fairy's entire attention turned
to musty, delicious-smelling mushrooms, a great abundance of which she
discovered at her feet, though she hadn't been able to see them from the air.
Although she really was hungry, she had to go on – after all, she was looking
for her wing!

In Futura City

The Serif Fairy already knew what cities looked like from above: great crowds of houses and people, streets, cars, and lights. To tell the truth, she really hadn't liked the cities very much. "But maybe I'll have some luck and find my wing there," she thought optimistically. So she got on the bus to Futura City.

In the city it was loud and hectic. The honking cars and the noise of the construction vehicles gave the Serif Fairy a headache. The commotion became too much for her, and she fled into a side street …

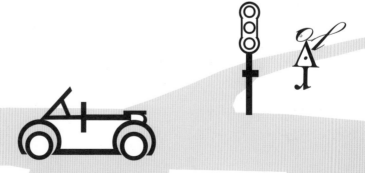

She came upon a large city square lined with tall houses. On one side of the square the Serif Fairy discovered a big building with a sign that read "Office of Lost Property." Her grandfather had told her that things found in the city were turned in there, and that hundreds of clocks, wallets, and umbrellas waited there to be picked up again by their owners. Would that work for her wing, too?

The Serif Fairy entered the building purposefully and addressed herself to a woman sitting behind a large desk. "Excuse me, did someone turn in a fairy wing?" asked the letter-fairy hopefully. "No, I'm sorry," said the woman and shook her head regretfully. The Serif Fairy left the building disappointed. She wanted to find some green space where she could rest a little.

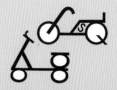

On Lake Shelley

The Serif Fairy ran out of the city hoping to find some nice greenery. She was glad to have left all the racket behind, and already she saw something silver glinting through the trees. Before her lay a lake, smooth and still. On the bank sat a fat, croaking frog. "A little refreshment would do me good. How are things, frog? Do you want to join me in the cool water?" she called. But the frog did not stir.

Suddenly a hissing water snake surfaced in front of the little letter-fairy. The Serif Fairy was so shocked that she fell backward. Her shock was so much greater than her fear of the water that she pulled herself together and jumped right into the lake with one hop. But the water snake didn't bother the Serif Fairy at all. It was just as shocked at seeing a letter-fairy for the first time …

Underwater, everything seemed to the Serif Fairy light and magical. The scales of the fish glinted, and swimming was almost as nice as flying. Deeper and deeper she dove into the clear, fresh water as algae tickled the end of her nose. Suddenly she noticed something glistening, fairy-like, hidden behind a big crab on the lake bottom. Full of curiosity, she dove deeper. At one point something brushed against her ear, but the little Serif Fairy never felt it again. But wait! What was that over there, glinting and twinkling? The Serif Fairy's heart beat harder and harder. Why, it was nothing other than her long sought-after, much-missed magic wing!

"My wing! Finally I found you!" rejoiced the Serif Fairy and stuck the wing right onto her shoulder. She wanted to swim quickly back up to the surface, but most of all she wanted to fly free of the water …

She surfaced, shook the water from her wings and lifted herself into the air. She flew higher and higher – she would never again touch the earth! She didn't even think about the fact that she was once again able to do magic. For now it was more than enough that she could fly. She left the lake behind and flew elatedly back over all the towns in which she had searched for her wing …

Throughout the book, small creatures have hidden themselves in places where they don't belong. Can you find them?

Aa

① Strokes of varying thickness, also called "heavy strokes."

② Little feet, also known as "serifs."

Garamond

ABCDEFGHIJKLMNOPQRSTUVWXYZ
abcdefghijklmnopqrstuvwxyz

① Large letters often have flourishes called "elephant trunks."

② The little feet are pointy. All letters stand on these points.

Zentenar-Fraktur

ABCDEFGHIJKLMNOPQRSTUVWXYZ
abcdefghijklmnopqrsstuvwxyz

1 Small little feet.

2 Uniform heavy strokes.

Futura Book

ABCDEFGHIJKLMNOPQRSTUVWXYZ
abcdefghijklmnopqrstuvwxyz

Letters look like they were written in calligraphy.

Shelley Andante Script

ABCDEFGHIJKLMNOPQRSTUVWXYZ
abcdefghijklmnopqrstuvwxyz

The Serif Fairy
Explorations in the World of Letters

Created as a studio work
for a course in communications design
at Muthesius Kunsthochschule, Kiel
4th semester, area of study conceived and designed
under the supervision of Profs. Silke Juchter and Klaus Detjen

Concept and design: René Siegfried

Original edition © 2006
Verlag Hermann Schmidt Mainz and by the author

Typescripts used:
Garamond, Zentenar-Fraktur, Futura Book,
Shelley Andante Script

Printing & binding through Asia Pacific Offset, Printed in China

English translation: Joel Mann
American edition production: Christopher D Salyers
American edition editing: Buzz Poole

First published in the United States of America in 2007 by
Mark Batty Publisher
36 W 37th St, Penthouse
New York, NY 10018
www.markbattypublisher.com

© 2007 Mark Batty Publisher LLC

Library of Congress Control Number:
2007922635

ISBN-10: 0-9790486-2-1
ISBN-13: 978-0-9790486-2-3

ejjorV

Garamond Forest

egVw

rVVV

rV

BBj

eJUV

cllOvvvww

AaacIIOo

ekoOw

Futura City

CCkQvY

GKKKnooopUUu

ACCloorT

ALllouy

kovY

HHlo

CCDJoot

abpry

ccDHVV